Lockdown

for

Lovers

For lonely hearts everywhere
and
my family, who make it all possible.

ISBN: 9798570342217

Lockdown

for

Lovers

Felicity Marris
with illustrations by Liz Haughton
and Felicity Marris

Look, look at the world today!
Look at this strange new world, I say!
At all the empty parks and streets,
and lonely hearts and itchy feet:
how all the people stay away –

I do not like this world, I say.
I want to go outside and play!

But Boris and his friends assert
that we must stay on high alert.

"Look now, look now, don't be fools!
With these rules,
and tools, we're coping
with the virus – Yes! we're hoping
that the Covid – nasty stuff –
will go away, we've had enough!"

In Lockdown, love is very tricky:
because this Covid is not picky
you cannot meet up for a quickie.

I do not like to live this way.
I do not like it, I must say!

I like to talk, I like to play,
I do not like my lonely day.

Some people live as man and wife
– and other forms of two by two –
and during Lockdown, muddle through,
in their own modes of love or strife.

But some live solo,
one by none,
and what then, what then,
can be done?

And what if you,
and your dear heart,
are newly met,
and live apart?

You may not like this separation,
but you must do it for the Nation!

And well you may, but your fun,
when it's done, can't be done in that way!

**B**ut look!
there are things you can safely do
to add one plus one to equal two.

You can Skype or Zoom,
in a virtual room.

You can queue in the street
to buy pasta to eat.

You can stand on the strand
where the water meets land.

You can go to the parks,
(but not the benches),
to talk and smile
are no offences.

But don't be hasty, you must be smart
and always stay quite far apart.
No holding hands or loving clinches,
the space between you: 80 inches.

But who will know,
I hear you say
And who will care, anyway?
I tell you there are those who will.
Yes, people who wish lovers ill...

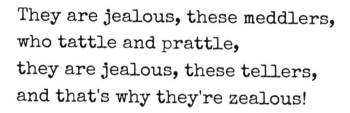

These are the dobbers,
the tellers, who tattle.
Proud to jump in
on your private battle.

They are jealous, these meddlers,
who tattle and prattle,
they are jealous, these tellers,
and that's why they're zealous!

So they'll fuss if you flirt
with your kissing and cuddling,
and they'll dob you for dabbling
in fondling and coupling.

ut here is a park with no one in!
Can we, can we, here, begin?

Or when it's dark,
may we have our fling?

Or here in the woods
we can hide in the trees
where no-one but wildlife
(and twitchers) can see.

And here is a beach
by the wild blue sea
– not a soul in sight –
do you think we might...?

This is hard, you say,
Oh say we may!

May we sit on the sand
just hand in hand?
May we lie on the stones
and entwine our bones?

There's no one for miles,
and we're not even ill.
This isolation's a bitter pill.

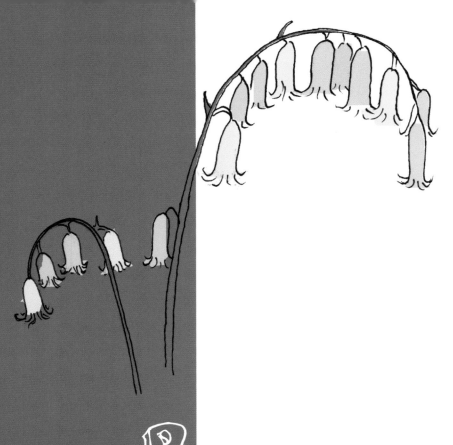

ut I must be clear!
The rules are stark:
You can walk and talk,
but your space musn't mingle.

Not in a park.
Not on the shingle.
Not in the dark.
Not in a dingle.

For if you dawdle in a dingle,
where the bluebell scents commingle
and your skin is set a-tingle
by your lover's dulcet jingle,

then the rule is clear, the rule is just,
the rule is that you really must
keep a check upon your lust.

And if you dandle, oh so nimble,
on the sand or on the shingle
for a fondle or canoodle
– let alone the whole caboodle...

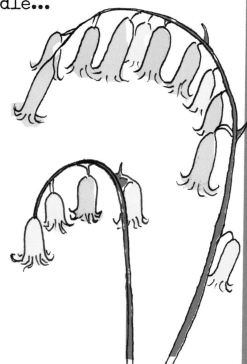

Then the tellers will start tattling
and police drones will start rattling
and it all gets quite unsettling
when the coppers interrupt you,
and insist that they disrupt you —
I can tell you, quite a muddle! —
In the middle of your cuddle,
when your lover's arms surround you,
and your clothes are strewn around you!

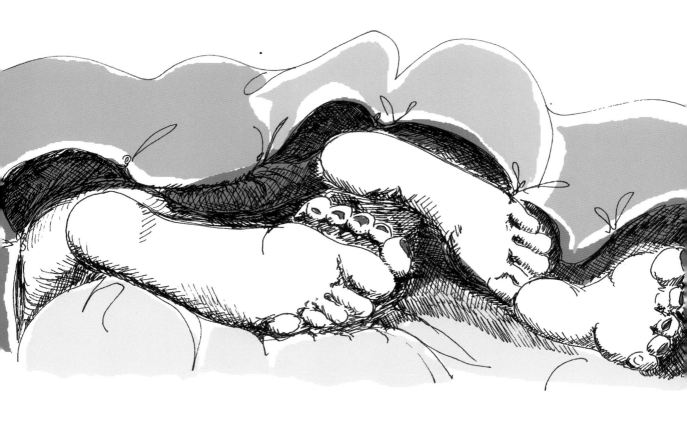

So, attempts to spoon canoodle
in a way that's rather rude'll
get you into deeper doodle
with the goons on lookout who'd all
rather you were single
in that lovely bluebell dingle.

But what if he asks me?
Yes, what if she asks – my lover –
to kiss, as we bask in the park?

In the space all around us
that's filling up fast
with people who start
rather far from their friends:
their mothers, and brothers,
and fathers and others,
who seem to be able to make metres bend?

You must never give in!
It's a new Covid sin
to be caught in a clinch
– you'll be lynched!

At last there are signs
of an end to these times,
when the Lockdown will all melt away.

But it's slow as you go,
for the lifting of woe,
though the rules changed again,
                        as you say.

So, to cut through the jargon,
you can visit in gardens,
just so long as you stand well away.
                    – hip hooray!

If we can walk through a house
(in the absence of spouse)
and sit on lawn, hammock or chair;

and if police can't come there,
to our private domain,
then surely my lover could come
... and remain?

We could stop in my house
on the way to the back,
we could lie on my bed,
we could cook up a snack...

No, no, no, I tell you again!
Begging your pardon,
but it's only the garden
where visitors can come through to sit.
And if it gets wet, there's no hiding inside.
Yes, if it gets wet, then that's it.

So not in a house?
And not in a bed?
But can we get tangled
in my shed here instead?

ot in a house!
Not in a bed!
Not in a garage!
Not in a shed!

No tangling and wrangling
Or any philandering,
All love is on hold for today.
And though you want fun,
your fun, when it's done,
just cannot be done in that way!

Save this fun for the day,
when the doctors all say
that full contact is back on the menu.
When Covid is beat,
we'll all kick up our feet,
and then you can roll in the hay!

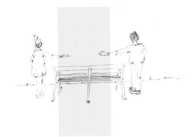

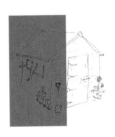

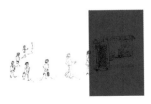

Acknowledgements

I would like to thank so many people for their input. Help and support has come from too many neighbours, friends, and family to mention individually, but a big thank you – you know who you are!

I would like to give a particular mention to Mania for telling me about KDP; to Al Powell at WriteClub for great advice; to BBC Radio Bristol for playing my recording; to Liz for her beautiful drawings, and Rosalind for putting us in touch; to Cornelia for her design help, and a quick shout of thanks to the providers of lovely free software and tutorials, especially Gimp and Scribus.

About the author

Felicity Marris has been writing, and pining, for too long for this to be the only output. She lives in Bristol with her four children.